T0116640

First published by Allen & Unwin in 2020

Copyright © Text, Anna Fienberg and Barbara Fienberg, 2020
Copyright © Illustrations, Kim Gamble, 1995–2017, and Kim Gamble, Arielle Gamble and Greer Gamble, 2020
All illustrations previously published by Allen & Unwin in various Tashi books from 1995–2017.

All rights reserved. No part of this book may be reproduced or transmitted in any form or by any means,
electronic or mechanical, including photocopying, recording or by any information storage and retrieval system,
without prior permission in writing from the publisher. The Australian *Copyright Act 1968* (the Act) allows
a maximum of one chapter or ten per cent of this book, whichever is the greater, to be photocopied by any
educational institution for its educational purposes provided that the educational institution (or body that
administers it) has given a remuneration notice to the Copyright Agency (Australia) under the Act.

Allen & Unwin
83 Alexander Street
Crows Nest NSW 2065
Australia
Phone: (61 2) 8425 0100
Email: info@allenandunwin.com
Web: www.allenandunwin.com

A catalogue record for this
book is available from the
National Library of Australia

ISBN 978 1 76052 528 6

For teaching resources, explore www.allenandunwin.com/resources/for-teachers

Illustration technique: Watercolour on paper

Cover and text design by Arielle Gamble
Set in Brandon Grotesque 32pt
This book was printed in January 2020 by Everbest Printing Co., Ltd, China

13 5 7 9 10 8 6 4 2

The paper in this book is FSC® certified.
FSC® promotes environmentally responsible,
socially beneficial and economically viable
management of the world's forests.

www.tashibooks.com

MY FIRST TASHI 123

Anna & Barbara Fienberg
Kim Gamble, Arielle & Greer Gamble

ALLEN&UNWIN

SYDNEY · MELBOURNE · AUCKLAND · LONDON

In this world of
caves and castles,
you can count…

One clever Tashi

Two sly demons

Three white tigers

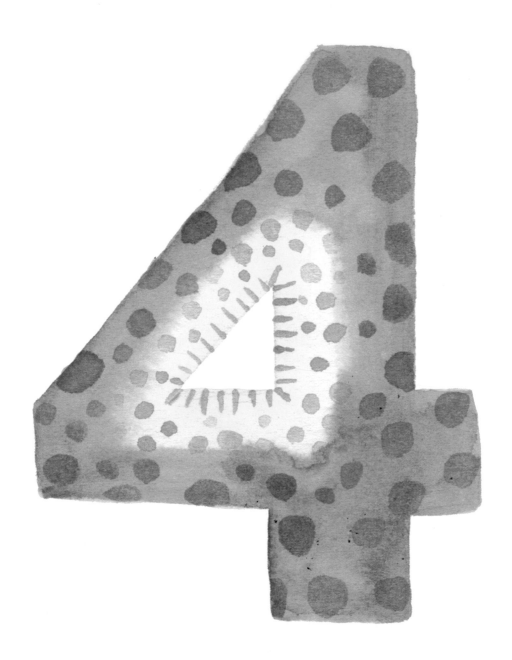

Four flaming dragons

Five round ogres

Six lazy genies

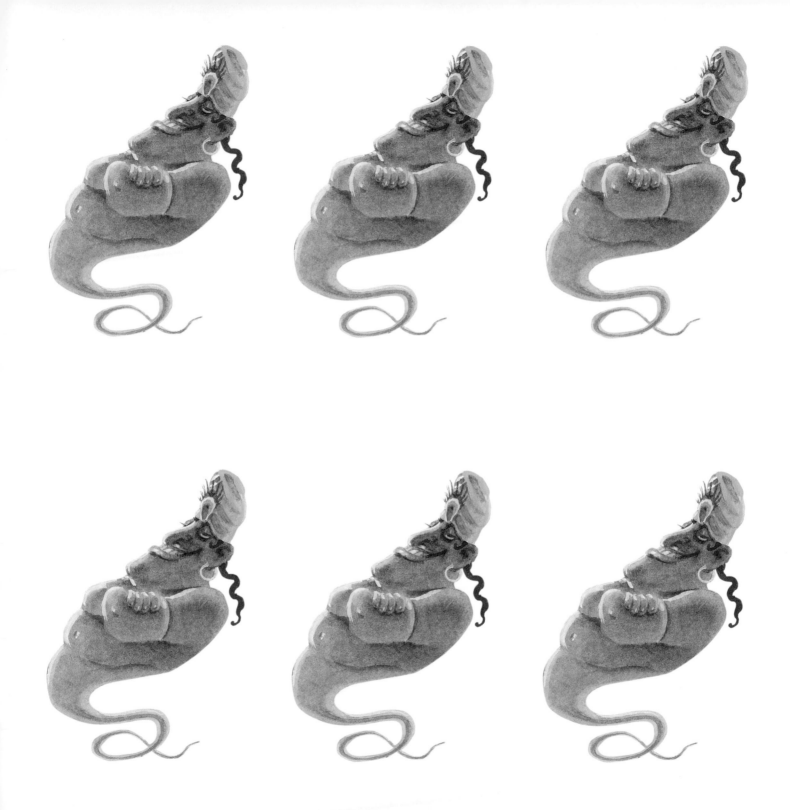

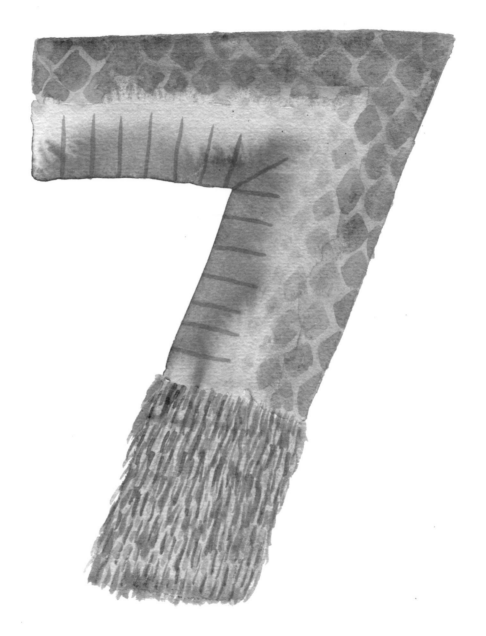

Seven mixed-up monsters

Eight flying phoenixes

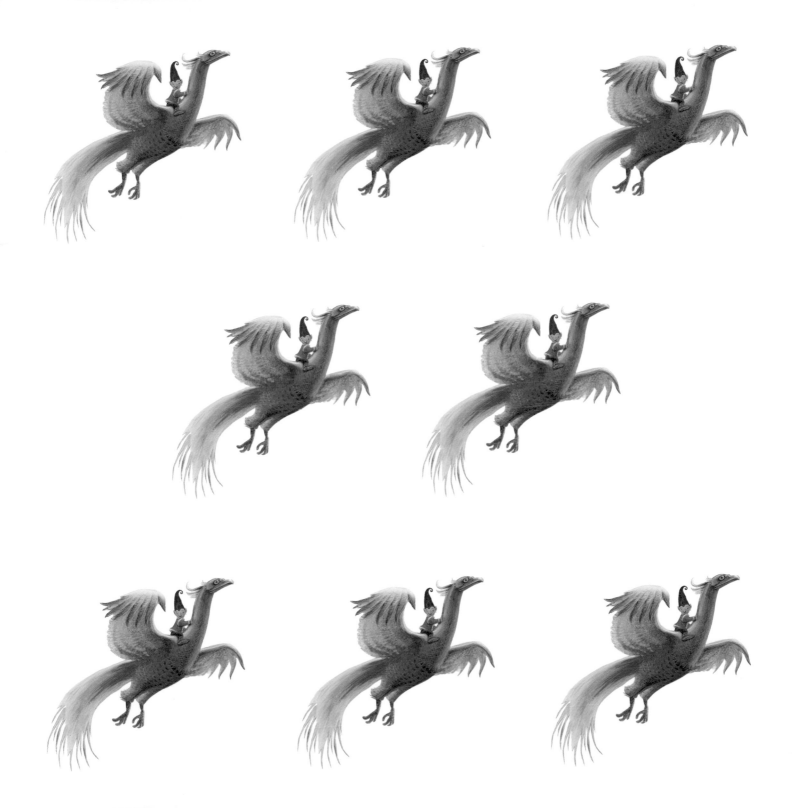

Nine yellow buses

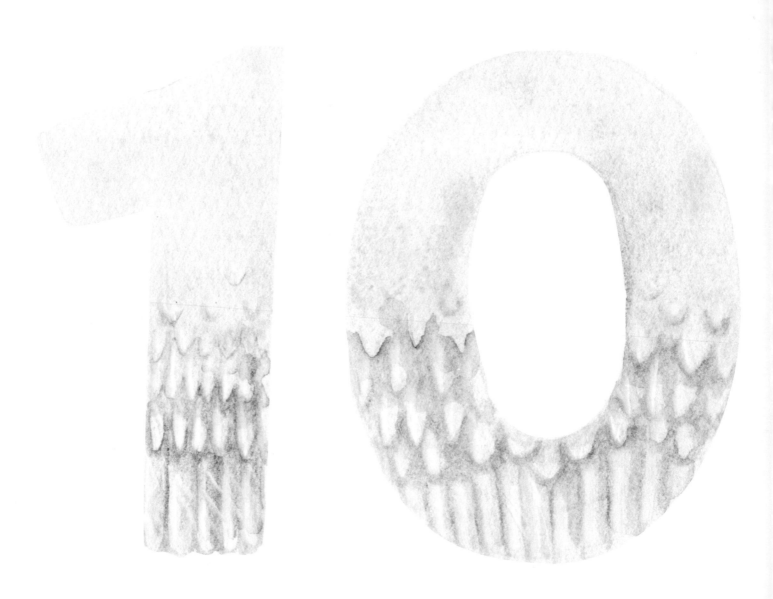

Ten swift swans

What else can you count at the fair?

ashi comes from two families, the Fienbergs and Gambles. My mother Barbara first saw him flying past on the back of a swan, so we brought him here to safety and gave him a best friend. And although Tashi told Jack the most marvellous tales, we didn't imagine Tashi would look very different from any other boy.

But when Kim Gamble got hold of him, Tashi turned from an ordinary boy who told magical tales into a magical boy. Kim shaped and dressed him, giving him a curious curl and a Santa Claus suit 'because Tashi carried magic gifts in his pockets'.

Tashi comes from a long line of storytellers. Since Barbara was very young, she told stories to entertain her friends (and get her out of trouble). And when she grew up to be a teacher librarian, she passed her passion for stories to me and hundreds of children as she read aloud to us in her library.

Kim too grew up loving stories, and drawing the heroes and baddies he found there. He also drew flowers when he couldn't contain his happiness. Kim and I met at *The School Magazine.* Our imaginations clicked and we went on to make scores of books. Like diving for a pearl, Kim reached in for the essence of a character, bringing it to the surface, extending feelings, transforming an idea into a world that was wilder and deeper than I'd ever realised.

I feel so lucky to have met this man, as do many thousands of children who've watched Kim draw a sunset, forests, moonlight over a river, all in the twenty minutes it took me to read the story.

And even though Kim is with us no longer, I am lucky that his exceptionally talented daughters have joined me now in Tashi's world. I've known and loved Arielle and Greer since they were little girls. From the time they were knee-high the girls' paintings hung amongst Kim's watercolours, blu-tacked up on his wall. As adults they've created their own paths across the artistic and literary landscape, and now they've brought their rich imaginations to join their father's, which has resulted in this truly family book.

We hope Tashi will become part of your family too.